Fairy Bears

Sparkle

"I promise to do my best. I promise to work hard to care for the world and all its plants, animals and children. This is the Fairy Bear Promise."

CANCELLED

C0000 002 537 373

Look out for more magical Fairy Bears!

Dizzy

Sunny

Blossom

Sparkle

Primrose

Misty

Lulu

Poppy

Visit the secret world of the Fairy Bears and
explore the magical Crystal Caves . . .

www.fairybearsworld.com

Fairy Bears

Sparkle

Julie Sykes

Illustrated by Samantha Chaffey

MACMILLAN CHILDREN'S BOOKS

First published 2010 by Macmillan Children's Books
a division of Macmillan Publishers Limited
20 New Wharf Road, London N1 9RR
Basingstoke and Oxford
Associated companies throughout the world
www.panmacmillan.com

ISBN 978-0-330-51204-6

Text copyright © Julie Sykes 2010
Illustrations copyright © Samantha Chaffey 2010

The right of Julie Sykes and Samantha Chaffey to be identified as the
author and illustrator of this work has been asserted by them in
accordance with the Copyright, Designs and Patents Act 1988.

All rights reserved. No part of this publication may be
reproduced, stored in or introduced into a retrieval system, or
transmitted, in any form or by any means (electronic, mechanical,
photocopying, recording or otherwise), without the prior written
permission of the publisher. Any person who does any unauthorized
act in relation to this publication may be liable to criminal
prosecution and civil claims for damages.

1 3 5 7 9 8 6 4 2

A CIP catalogue record for this book is available from
the British Library.

Printed and bound in the UK by CPI Mackays, Chatham ME5 8TD

This book is sold subject to the condition that it shall not,
by way of trade or otherwise, be lent, resold, hired out,
or otherwise circulated without the publisher's prior consent
in any form of binding or cover other than that in which
it is published and without a similar condition including this
condition being imposed on the subsequent purchaser.

For William

Prologue

At the bottom of Firefly Meadow, not far from the stream, stands a tall sycamore tree. The tree is old with a thick grey trunk and spreading branches. Hidden amongst the branches is a forgotten squirrel hole. If you could fly through the squirrel hole and down the inside of the tree's hollow trunk, you would find a secret door that leads to a special place. Open the door and step inside the magical Crystal Caves, home of the Fairy Bears.

The Fairy Bears are always busy. They work hard caring for nature and children everywhere. You'll have to be quick to see them, and you'll have to believe in magic.

Fairy Bears

Do you believe in Fairy Bear magic?
Can you keep a secret? Then come on in –
the Fairy Bears would love to meet you.

Chapter One

Sparkle was about to enter her class cave when another Fairy Bear with brightly glittering wings fluttered past. Hardly able to believe her eyes, Sparkle stopped. She would do anything for wings like that! Impulsively she called out, "You look beautiful. How did you make your wings glitter?"

The Fairy Bear turned round and Sparkle held her breath, recognizing her as an older Fairy Bear called April. Would she be too grand to speak to a mere junior like

herself? April
smiled then
modestly
fluttered
her wings.
"Thank
you. Mum
stuck jewels
on my wings
with magic
for a birthday
treat."

Sparkle stared at April's twinkling wings
until she reached the end of the tunnel and
disappeared round the corner.

"Hello, Sparkle, what are you doing out
here? Hurry up inside. I'm sending someone
on their first task today," said Miss Alaska
as she swept past Sparkle and entered the
class cave. Eagerly Sparkle followed her.

Sparkle Saves the Day

Fairy Bears started taking tasks in the last year of juniors and had to pass them all before they were allowed to move up to the senior classes. The tasks were really important and usually involved helping someone or the environment they lived in. Sparkle hadn't done any tasks yet and was longing to go out on her first one.

Please let Miss Alaska choose me, she thought as she sat down next to her friend Blossom.

"Hello," whispered Blossom. "You were almost late."

"I know," said Sparkle, putting her wand on the table and neatly closing her red wings. "Guess what I saw!"

Blossom put a paw to her lips shushing Sparkle as Miss Alaska started to call the register. Sparkle wriggled impatiently. She wanted to tell Blossom about April's wings.

When Miss Alaska had finished, she held up a large green sycamore leaf. An excited murmur rippled round the class and Sparkle sat up straight, April's wings suddenly forgotten.

"It's task time again," said Miss Alaska. "But first let's say the Fairy Bear Promise."

Stones scraped on the class cave floor as the Fairy Bears stood up and joined paws. Sparkle had Blossom on one side of her and Primrose on the other. Excitedly she clutched their paws. Would it be her turn to go out on a task? She hoped so!

"I promise to do my best. I promise to work hard to care for the world and all its plants, animals and children. This is the Fairy Bear Promise," Sparkle chanted earnestly. She stared at Miss Alaska, hoping she would be chosen.

Miss Alaska looked at the sycamore leaf.

"This task is for Sparkle," she announced.

Wings trembling with delight, Sparkle took the leaf to find out what her task was.

"Guess what!" she said, her brown eyes shining as she read the task. "I'm to help a colony of butterflies. They're living on a piece of wasteland in the middle of a town, but developers are about to build houses on it so they need to find a new home."

At the bottom of the task was a map. The town was a long way from the sycamore tree. Sparkle couldn't believe her good luck. She loved pretty creatures like butterflies and she loved flying too.

"Poor you," said Coral, who was known for her sharp tongue. "The beautiful butterflies will make you look quite plain, Sparkle."

Sparkle's wings drooped and she stared at Coral in dismay.

"The tasks are about helping others, Coral," said Miss Alaska sternly. "Sparkle isn't plain but she'll be too busy helping the butterflies to worry about her looks."

The class giggled, knowing that Sparkle was very particular about her appearance. Her fur shone from constant combing and she loved pretty things. As Sparkle walked to the door, she sneaked a look in the magic mirror. At first a pretty bear with gleaming gold fur and bright red wings stared back. Then in a swirl of silver the picture changed. Sparkle held her breath, wondering what she would see next. The magic mirror didn't always show reflections. Sometimes it showed things that were magical or useful. As the new picture became clearer, Sparkle saw an overgrown patch of land bursting with wildflowers and butterflies.

"Oh," she sighed, leaning closer so her nose almost touched the mirror's surface. "They're beautiful."

In a flash of silver the butterflies were replaced by a picture of a grimy street littered with empty food wrappers and drinks cans. Sparkle gasped at the contrast. This road was horrible. A stream of cars rumbled alongside the pavement where an athletic-looking girl was walking. Her light brown hair was held back by a brightly-coloured headband with *Isabel* stitched across the top. Her shoulders were bent with the weight of the large school bag she carried on her back.

"Poor Isabel," murmured Sparkle. "I'm not surprised she looks fed up."

Sparkle loved children and was disappointed that her task wasn't to help Isabel. But the mirror was changing again and Isabel was replaced by the butterflies. Captivated, Sparkle soon forgot Isabel as she watched the butterflies dancing in the air. As the picture faded away, Sparkle sighed. It didn't matter that Miss Alaska had said that tasks were about helping others – the beautiful butterflies still made her feel plain. Sadly she wrapped the sycamore leaf with her task written on round her wand and flew from the

class cave. Sparkle was halfway across
the playground when a wonderful idea
occurred to her. Flying faster, she headed
home.

Chapter Two

"Mum," called Sparkle, rushing indoors. "Can I borrow your diamonds?"

The Crystal Caves were full of sparkling jewels. Fairy Bears used them to decorate their homes on special occasions. Sparkle's mum was very fond of diamonds and had a large collection.

"Hello, dear." Sparkle's grandma poked her head out of the living cave.

"Grandma," squealed Sparkle, rushing forward and hugging her. "What a lovely surprise."

"And for me too," said Grandma, her silver wings quivering with delight. "Your mum asked me to look after Fizz while she popped out. Why aren't you at school?"

"I'm going on my first task," said Sparkle. Excitedly she told Grandma about

the butterflies, adding, "I came home to ask Mum if I could borrow her diamonds to make my wings look pretty. Can I, Grandma? Will you stick them to my wings for me?"

Grandma's face clouded. "I don't know, Sparkle. They're not mine to lend."

"Please, Grandma. Mum often lets me borrow her things," Sparkle begged.

"Mummy lend 'Parkle diamonds," said Fizz, tottering towards her big sister.

Sparkle held her breath. It sounded like Fizz was saying that Mum had lent Sparkle the diamonds before. Grandma hesitated. "Please, 'Anma," said Fizz. "Mummy let 'Parkle."

"Well, if you're sure Mum won't mind, then you can," she said eventually.

"Thanks!" squealed Sparkle, hugging Grandma then scooping up Fizz to hug her

too. "I promise I'll look after them. Will you stick them on for me?"

It took much longer than Sparkle had thought to magically stick her mum's diamonds to her wings but when Grandma had finished they both agreed it was worth the effort. Grandma made Sparkle do a twirl.

"You look beautiful," she sighed.

"Pretty 'Parkle," cooed Fizz, clapping her paws in delight.

"I can't wait to meet the butterflies," said Sparkle happily. They would have to like her now!

Unused to the extra weight of the diamonds, Sparkle held her wings stiffly as she flew to the Grand Door. It was mid-morning so the tunnels were empty. Sparkle was disappointed that there was no one to see her but relieved that she hadn't been caught in the early morning crush, as that might have ruined her wings. The Grand Door was closed. After climbing the gnarled root staircase, Sparkle reached for the leaf-shaped door handle. Twisting it round, she pushed the door open and stepped inside the tree trunk. The diamonds on Sparkle's wings twinkled magically in the dark. Sparkle was ecstatic.

"I want diamonds on my wings every day!" she exclaimed.

Excitedly Sparkle leaped into the air. She loved the way the jewels made her wings glitter and was so busy admiring them she nearly flew past the squirrel hole. Stopping with a jerk, Sparkle anxiously checked that all her mum's diamonds were still in place. Satisfied she hadn't lost any, Sparkle flew outside and landed on a branch to study her map.

At first Sparkle enjoyed her long flight to town. The sunlight made her wings shine more brightly than usual and she saw two butterflies and a bumblebee stare at her as she flew by. She was surprised when she tired more quickly than usual but soon realized it was the diamonds making her wings feel heavy.

"Not far now," said Sparkle firmly, resisting the urge to stop for a rest.

She was very glad when the landscape changed from neat green fields to sprawling rows of houses. Sparkle flew down to a street lamp and perched on the top to check

her map again. It was such a relief to rest
her wings that Sparkle studied the map for
longer than she needed to. At last it was
time to go. Rolling the sycamore leaf back
round her wand, Sparkle set off on the final
part of her journey. She flew over a school,
its playground crowded with noisy children,
and there on the corner of the next street
was an overgrown patch of land.

"That's it!" cried Sparkle.

Quickly she flew along the street. It was
as dirty and noisy as the one she'd seen
in the magic mirror. Sparkle shuddered,
wishing that her task could have been
somewhere nicer. At the corner she flew
between two sprawling bushes and into
the wasteland then stopped in surprise. It
was lovely here. Hidden from the road by
overgrown bushes, the area was a riot of
coloured wildflowers, nettles and bushes.

Sparkle breathed deeply, enjoying the sweet scent of nectar as she hovered overhead. The flowers were twitching and fluttering as if they'd magically come to life. Sparkle stared, then realized that it wasn't the flowers moving. It was butterflies. They were everywhere, darting from plant to plant on their beautiful wings.

Suddenly Sparkle was overcome with shyness. The butterflies were much bigger than her and they were all so pretty. Nervously she ran a paw through her fur and then checked her wings. The diamonds flashed miniature rainbows in the sunlight, making Sparkle's red wings twinkle. She flushed with pleasure.

Reassured that she looked good enough to meet the butterflies, Sparkle flew down and landed on a yellow-headed daisy. It smelt delicious. Thirsty after her long

flight, Sparkle had a long drink of nectar.
A butterfly with red wings and four brightly
coloured spots landed nearby. It was about
to drink some nectar when it noticed
Sparkle's diamonds. One of its antennae
twitched in surprise. Shyly Sparkle dipped
a wing. The butterfly dipped a wing back
then fluttered closer. Sparkle did a slow
twirl, so the beautiful butterfly could see

how pretty her wings were. The butterfly clicked a greeting.

"Hello," Sparkle softly answered.

Another butterfly with bright blue wings edged with black and white flew over. She was followed by an orange butterfly, with pretty black and blue markings. Soon the air was alive with butterflies, crowding round Sparkle. She basked in all the attention until a pearly white butterfly cheekily tapped his enormous wing against hers. Sparkle wished she could understand the butterfly, but talking to animals wasn't taught until the seniors.

"Plink?" she asked, thinking of the chasing game they played at home.

The butterfly tapped Sparkle again then slowly flew away, checking to see she was following. Satisfied that she was, the butterfly sped up, dipping and diving each time Sparkle tried to tap him back. The other butterflies joined in and Sparkle raced through the air with them, sometimes chasing and sometimes being chased. This was the best game of Plink she'd played in ages! The butterflies were fast and Sparkle had to work hard to keep up with them. Eventually Sparkle sank down on the soft head of a purple knapweed to get her breath back and have another drink.

"Truce," she panted.

Quizzically a blue butterfly landed next to her. Sparkle rested her head on her paw, closing her eyes to show the butterfly she was tired. Something fell to the ground with a chink. Sparkle opened her eyes. What was that? The blue butterfly pointed his antennae at her wing. Thinking he was admiring her again, Sparkle dipped her wings back.

"Thank you," she said.

The butterfly shook his head and
pointed his antennae
again.

Sparkle peered
over her shoulder at
her wings.

"Oh no!" she
gasped.

Where had all Mum's
diamonds gone? Sparkle

tried to count the diamonds left on her
wings. From the gaps she guessed she'd lost
half of her mum's precious jewels.

Chapter Three

Sparkle's wings went ice cold. She'd promised to be careful with the diamonds and now she'd lost them. Mum would be furious. And what about Grandma? Would she be in trouble too? The blue butterfly was tapping his wing against Sparkle's as if he wanted her to follow him. Sparkle flew after him to the ground and there under the knapweed was a diamond. Gratefully she pounced on it.

"Thank you," she said.

The blue butterfly nodded his head then

called out to his friends. Immediately the butterflies stopped chasing each other and crowded round. The butterfly spoke to his friends in clicks and squeaks then they all began searching for the missing diamonds. Each time they found a diamond the butterfly tapped Sparkle on the wing and showed her where it was. Sparkle couldn't hold all the diamonds in her paws and look for more at the same time so she made a pile under a bush.

The butterflies searched for ages until there were only a few diamonds left to find. Eventually they drifted away until only the blue butterfly was left. Sparkle flew alongside him, searching the remaining patch of ground. Where were the last few diamonds? She had to find them quickly so that she could start on her task. Sparkle had been so busy having fun she'd forgotten that the butterflies were about to lose their home.

Suddenly everything went black. Sparkle's heart thumped wildly as she spun through the air, trapped inside a cave with soft, warm walls. This was terrifying. What had happened to her? Then the walls of the cave opened. As the light poured in, Sparkle waited for a chance to escape, but a girl's voice whispered, "Hello. Are you some kind of fairy?"

With a start Sparkle realized she was standing on a girl's cupped hand. The girl was staring at her with amazement. Sparkle stared back, taking in her light brown hair held back with a hairband. She knew this girl. It was Isabel, from the picture in the magic mirror.

"Hello, Isabel," said Sparkle. "I'm not a fairy – I'm a Fairy Bear."

"A Fairy Bear!" Isabel's pale blue eyes popped with excitement. "How do you know my name?" she asked.

Smiling shyly Sparkle pointed to Isabel's headband. Isabel chuckled then said, "Do you live here? How come I've never seen you before? I've come here every day on my way home from school since we moved. We used to live in the country, but then

Dad lost his job and he could only find a new one in town. Mum's got a new job too. It's lonely going home to an empty house. That's why I come here. This patch of land reminds me of our old home." Isabel stopped talking and blushed. "Sorry, I always talk too much."

"I'm here to help the butterflies," said Sparkle. "This land is going to be built on so I have to find the butterflies a new home."

Isabel's face fell.

"I heard about that from Dad. I've been trying not to think about it. Where are you going to move the butterflies to?"

Sparkle's wings quivered sadly.

"I'm not sure yet. I've lost some things that didn't belong to me and I have to find them before I can help the butterflies."

"I'm good at looking for things," said

Isabel eagerly. "What have you lost?"

"My mum's diamonds," said Sparkle.

"Diamonds!" Isabel was shocked and impressed. "Your mum let you borrow her diamonds?"

"Sort of," said Sparkle. She stared at her paws, suddenly ashamed of herself. She hadn't been exactly truthful when she'd persuaded Grandma to let her take the jewels.

"Where do you think you lost them?" said Isabel, dumping her school bag on the ground.

Isabel was very thorough. With her eyes glued to the ground she walked in a line across the patch of wasteland, then, reaching the end, walked back. Up and down she went, bending each time she spotted something glittering in the sunlight.

"They're so tiny," she said, staring at the

miniature diamond in her cupped hand.

There were lots of false alarms but Isabel kept searching until all the diamonds had been recovered. Sparkle couldn't stop thanking her.

"How are you going to get them home
– do you have a bag?" asked Isabel. She
stared at the pile of jewels glittering in the
sunlight.

Sparkle hadn't thought about that. There
was no way she could magically stick the
jewels back on her wings without help.
She could just about carry them but it
would make flying difficult and what if she
accidentally dropped one? She did need a
bag.

Thoughtfully Sparkle twiddled her wand;
it was very pretty, gold in colour with a
cluster of tiny red rubies set in the star.
Sparkle was good at magic but she couldn't
magic up a bag from nothing. Maybe there
was something on the wasteland she could
use to make a bag from . . . She stared
around but the only thing she could see was
Isabel's enormous school bag. It was perfect!

31

She could easily shrink that to Fairy Bear size if Isabel would lend it to her.

"Where do you live?" asked Isabel. "Can I help you to carry the diamonds home?"

Sparkle didn't answer. She was having a brilliant idea. It meant trusting Isabel but Sparkle sensed that she would be good at keeping secrets.

Wings trembling with excitement, she said, "I live in the Crystal Caves. It's a long way from here. If you really don't mind helping me take the diamonds home, then you could visit. It would mean shrinking you down to my size, though."

"R-r-really?" stuttered Isabel, her pale blue eyes shining. "Would I have wings as well?"

Isabel's enthusiasm was catching and made Sparkle laugh.

"Of course," she said.

"Go on, then." Isabel stood very still. "Shrink me now."

"Hold on to your bag," said Sparkle. "We'll need it to carry the diamonds back and I'm not sure if I can do two shrinking spells in a row."

Isabel snatched up her bag as Sparkle experimentally waved her wand. The cluster of rubies flashed in the sunlight as Sparkle chanted:

"Shrink Isabel down as small as a bee
Then give her wings just like me."

33

The wand trembled. Sparkle held her breath. It was a complicated spell. Would she have enough energy to make the magic work?

Chapter Four

The wand vibrated, slowly at first then faster and faster. The cluster of rubies glowed and the gold star shone like the sun. Sparkle gripped the wand tightly as with a loud pop a river of sparkling red stars burst from its tip. They rained over Isabel, making her skin and hair glitter.

"Oh!" squeaked Isabel, her eyes widening. "I feel funny."

Isabel was shrinking. Her voice faded as her body became tinier. Red stars popped and fizzed at Isabel's back then disappeared in a glittering swirl of red. Sparkle clapped her paws with delight. That had been hard work but she'd done it! She'd shrunk Isabel to the same size as herself. For a moment no one spoke then the tiny Isabel threw herself at Sparkle and hugged her tight.

"Thank you," she gabbled. "Just look at me. I'm like a fairy. Look at my lovely wings."

Isabel twirled round, showing off the beautiful butterfly-shaped wings sprouting from her back.

"They're the same colour as yours," she said proudly.

"Almost," said Sparkle enviously, noticing that Isabel's wings had streaks of gold that shimmered in the sunlight.

Frowning with concentration, Isabel fluttered her wings. "I can fly!" she cried.

"Look, Sparkle, I'm flying!"

"Well done." Sparkle clapped loudly as Isabel flew in a circle. "Take bigger wing strokes. That's it, now you're not wobbling!"

"This is brilliant fun," cried Isabel, changing direction.

"Are you ready to fly home with me or do you want more practice?" asked Sparkle.

"Let's go now," said Isabel. Confidently she landed next to Sparkle and together they placed the diamonds safely in the bag.

"I can't wait to see your home!" said Isabel excitedly.

Sparkle and Isabel flew side by side, carrying Isabel's bag between them.

"Flying is brilliant," said Isabel, her eyes sparkling, as they flew over the green

countryside. As Firefly Meadow drew closer Sparkle felt a sharp pang of worry. What would Mum say when she returned the diamonds? Would she be cross with Sparkle for persuading Grandma to let her take them? And what about her task? She hadn't even started it yet! Sparkle suddenly felt very guilty.

Approaching the sycamore tree, Sparkle

saw two Fairy Bears sitting amongst its leaves. She was relieved that they were too busy talking to notice her new friend fly in through the squirrel hole. Suddenly Sparkle was worried about bringing Isabel back to the Crystal Caves. It wasn't something that happened very often. All Sparkle wanted to do was return Mum's diamonds and get started with her task.

Sparkle held on to Isabel's hand as they flew in the darkness to the bottom of the tree but Isabel wasn't scared of the dark.

"This is brilliant," sighed Isabel. "It reminds me of night-time in the country. It doesn't get properly dark in the town because of all the street lights."

Isabel was amazed by the Grand Door.

"It's enormous," she cried. "And I love the leaf-shaped handle."

They flew down the gnarled root staircase

and along the main tunnel.

"Slower!" begged Isabel, gazing with awe at the glittering walls.

Sparkle laughed as she slowed down. She was anxious to return her mum's diamonds but it was such fun sharing her home with Isabel. It made her see the Crystal Caves with new eyes. Suddenly she was very glad she lived in such an amazing place. At the diamond archway that marked the entrance to the Royal Tunnel Isabel stopped in mid-air.

"That's so beautiful," she gasped. "Where does it lead to?"

Sparkle hesitated. The Royal Tunnel led to the Royal Caves, home of King Boris and Queen Tania. Fairy Bears were allowed as far as the spectacular Butterfly Bridge that crossed the underground stream. It was one of the prettiest places in the

Crystal Caves and Sparkle longed to show Isabel. Deciding the diamonds would be safe in Isabel's bag for a while longer, she made a detour under the archway.

"That's the most amazing bridge I've ever seen," said Isabel, unable to take her eyes off the jewel-studded bridge shaped like a butterfly.

The stream gurgled cheerfully beneath the bridge. Isabel sat on the bank and dipped her hands in the crystal-clear water.

"Careful you don't get your wings wet," warned Sparkle. "It's impossible to fly with wet wings."

"This reminds me of my old home," said Isabel wistfully. "We had a stream at the bottom of our garden. We've hardly got any garden now. Half of it is patio and the rest is scrubby grass with a border of weeds.

Mum and Dad keep saying they'll tidy it up but they're always too busy working."

"Maybe you could do it for them," suggested Sparkle.

Isabel let her hand drift in the ice-cold water.

"Perhaps," she said thoughtfully.

It wasn't far from the Royal Tunnel to Sparkle's cave but it took ages to get there. Isabel kept stopping to admire the jewels in the walls and Isabel begged Sparkle to take her to see the school caves. The Fairy Bears were all in lessons so Sparkle took Isabel for a quick fly round the empty playground.

"I'd love to go inside the class caves," said Isabel longingly.

"That would give everyone a surprise," giggled Sparkle.

As they were leaving the school, Isabel

spotted the entrance to the Crystal Maze on the opposite side of the tunnel and flitted over.

"Don't go in," warned Sparkle, hurrying after her. "If you take a wrong turning, you'll be lost inside for ages."

"It's beautiful," sighed Isabel, reaching out to touch the colourful column of crystal decorating the maze's entrance.

Sparkle couldn't help laughing at Isabel's excitement.

"You're a bad influence," she joked. "Mum's always complaining that I'm easily distracted and you're making me worse. Come on, I have to take these diamonds back before I lose them again."

Reluctantly Isabel left the Crystal Maze and followed Sparkle. As they grew nearer to Sparkle's home, Isabel fell silent as if lost in her thoughts.

"We're here," said Sparkle, hesitating at her front door.

Isabel hovered beside her. "Look at your front door. It's so pretty. Do all doors have jewels on them?"

Sparkle nodded. "Every door is different."

"Our old house had a name, Bracken Cottage, but our new house has a boring old number," said Isabel wistfully.

Now that the moment had come to return Mum's diamonds Sparkle was very nervous.

"Would you mind waiting here?" she asked Isabel. "In case Mum's cross with me."

"Of course I don't mind," said Isabel. "Shall I wait in that tiny cave over there?"

"That's a great idea," said Sparkle, relieved that Isabel wasn't upset.

Isabel emptied the diamonds out of her school bag and into Sparkle's arms, then hurried along the tunnel to the cave. Hugging the diamonds close to her chest, Sparkle carried them indoors.

"Hello," she called out. "Is anyone home?"

Her heart was banging nervously. Would Mum tell her and Grandma off for taking the diamonds?

"Shhh!" whispered Grandma, appearing from Fizz's cave. "Your sister has just fallen asleep."

"Grandma!" whispered Sparkle, relieved

that her mum wasn't back yet. She hung her head, staring at her paws. "I've got something to tell you."

"You've lost some of your mum's diamonds," said Grandma flatly.

"I did lose some but I found them again. But I wasn't very honest. Mum has never lent me her diamonds before."

Wordlessly Grandma reached out and took the diamonds from Sparkle.

"I'm sorry," Sparkle whispered, her red wings drooping miserably.

Surprisingly Grandma smiled.

"That wasn't a nice thing to do, but I'm pleased you realized your mistake and had the courage to own up." She reached out and softly stroked Sparkle's wing with her own silver one.

"Come on," she said kindly. "Let's put the diamonds away before Mum gets back.

I know you won't do this again. You've learned your lesson."

Chapter Five

Sparkle and Isabel flew out of the squirrel hole and across Firefly Meadow.

"I don't want this to end," said Isabel, flying slower. "I love the Crystal Caves and I love flying."

"Your parents would miss you if you didn't go back," said Sparkle, swerving to avoid colliding with a wasp.

"Ugh!" shuddered Isabel. "That wasp was enormous! Maybe there are advantages to being big. And, yes, my parents would miss me. I'd miss them too."

She checked her watch and sighed.

"We'll have to hurry. Mum and Dad will be back from work soon."

"I can't wait to see where you live," said Sparkle.

"It's not as exciting as your home," said Isabel. "It's on a busy road and the garden's tiny."

Soon Sparkle saw exactly what Isabel meant. She lived in a tall house with wide stone steps leading straight up from the pavement. Small patio pots containing half-dead weeds were arranged on either side of the stairs and empty window boxes hung from the downstairs windows. As they approached the house, Isabel began to giggle.

"We'll have to fly over the side gate and into the back garden," she said. "I can't get in until you turn me back to my proper size.

Look at my front-door key. It won't fit the
lock any more."

Isabel reached inside her school polo shirt
and pulled out a piece of ribbon hanging
round her neck. Dangling from the ribbon
was a tiny silver key.

"Whoops!" chuckled Sparkle. "I forgot you use keys. We use magic to lock our front doors."

"That's so cool," Isabel sighed.

Isabel's back garden was exactly as she'd described it. Sparkle could see why Isabel stopped off at the patch of wasteland every day. It was much prettier there. She landed in the far corner next to a tiny garden shed and Isabel reluctantly landed beside her.

"That was so much fun," she said.

Sparkle pointed her wand at Isabel. "Ready?"

"I suppose so," said Isabel, fluttering her red-gold wings one last time.

Waving her wand Sparkle chanted:

"Wand before my very eyes
Return Isabel to her proper size."

53

The wand trembled. Sparkle held on tight as a stream of glittering red stars shot out from the end, covering Isabel.

"Ooh!" Isabel squealed. "That tickles!"

She giggled as the stars fizzled away on her skin, her voice growing louder as she returned to her normal height.

"Phew!" she said when the magic had finished. "Thank goodness the magic knew when to stop or I might have ended up like a giant."

In the distance a door slammed and Isabel said, "Sounds like my mum's home. The time after school normally drags, but not today. It's flown!" she added, chuckling at her own joke.

The back door opened and a tired-looking lady wearing a crumpled suit poked her head out.

"There you are, Isabel. How did you get

into the garden without unlocking the back door?"

"Hi, Mum. I came in through the side gate," said Isabel truthfully. "I have to go," she whispered to Sparkle. "Thanks for a brilliant time. I hope I see you again soon."

As Isabel hurried indoors, Sparkle took another look around her garden. Poor Isabel! It must be hard for her to settle here when she was used to open countryside.

"Honey mites!" exclaimed Sparkle suddenly. The butterflies! She had to help them before they became homeless and she failed her task. But it was too late to do anything now. It was early evening. Sparkle had to go home before dark or she would fail her task anyway. Quickly she flew back to the Crystal Caves, wondering how to help the butterflies. The only thing she could think of was to persuade them to move to the country. But somehow that didn't feel like the right solution. Arriving back at the Crystal Caves, Sparkle was surprised to see Miss Alaska waiting for her at the bottom of the gnarled root staircase.

"Hello, Sparkle. How did you get on?"

Sparkle hesitated. She'd had a great time playing with the butterflies, meeting Isabel and showing her the Crystal Caves, but she didn't think Miss Alaska would be interested in hearing about that.

"I found the butterflies," she said, "but I'm not sure how to help them."

"Hmmm," said Miss Alaska, writing something in her leaf note book. "Did something distract you from your task?"

56

Sparkle flushed. "There's nowhere to move the butterflies to," she answered, avoiding the question. "The town is so dirty and ugly."

"Is it?" Miss Alaska sounded surprised. "Have you explored it properly? Looks aren't everything, Sparkle. You need to find out what things are like on the inside. I suggest that tomorrow you stop fussing about appearances and get on with the job."

Sparkle's wings twitched uncomfortably as Miss Alaska fixed her with a long stare. It was a good thing she didn't know about the diamonds or she would have been even crosser.

"I will," she whispered, promising herself that tomorrow would be different.

The following morning Sparkle left the Crystal Caves early and flew to town.

Instead of going to visit the butterflies she decided that first she would find a new home for them. Remembering how thorough Isabel had been when searching for the lost diamonds Sparkle followed her example, flying up and down the streets, looking for somewhere for the butterflies to live.

There were a couple more patches of wasteland but Sparkle didn't want to move the butterflies there in case that land was also going to be built on soon. She found a play park but there were no plants, just play equipment and benches for people to sit on. Its bareness reminded Sparkle of Isabel's garden and it gave her an idea.

She fluttered down and rested on the top of the swings while she thought it through. If her plan worked, it would be good for both the butterflies and Isabel. Sparkle couldn't wait to put her plan into action, but first she needed Isabel's permission.

Excitedly she flew towards the wasteland to wait for Isabel to visit. But as she got closer a small doubt began to nag at her. What if Isabel didn't stop off at the wasteland on her way home from school? Sparkle couldn't leave it to chance. The builders might start work any day. She had to speak to Isabel before it was too late! Then she had another good idea. Isabel had visited Sparkle's school, so why didn't she visit Isabel at hers?

Chapter Six

Arriving at Isabel's school, Sparkle was
surprised to see a crowd of adults outside the
gates. She hadn't realized it was home time
already. She looked around for somewhere
to wait for Isabel and found a metal school
sign to perch on. Seconds later a sea of red-
and-grey clothed children streamed out of
the school buildings. Sparkle leaned forward,
trying to spot Isabel. There! Eagerly she
flew towards the mousey-haired girl. But
it wasn't Isabel, and the girl screamed and
flapped at Sparkle, thinking she was a bee.

"Stay calm," called a parent. "Look, the bee's flying away."

"Too right!" yelped Sparkle, speeding in the opposite direction.

"Eeek!" squealed a boy, swatting her as she flew past. "It tried to sting me."

Sparkle was too frightened to be indignant. Her wings were trembling so badly she could hardly fly.

"Sparkle," hissed a voice. "Over here."

Isabel! Relieved Sparkle dashed towards her friend and, landing on her shoulder, hid under her hair.

Isabel quickened her pace, leaving behind the noisy children.

"You can come out now," she said, once they were safely on the wasteland.

"Thanks." Sparkle fluttered out of hiding and rested on Isabel's hand.

Isabel's cheeks turned pink with pleasure.

"How come everyone thought you were a bee?" she giggled.

Sparkle combed her ruffled fur.

"We're the same size, we're both furry and we both have wings. It's an easy mistake to make if you don't believe in magic."

"How can you not believe in magic?" Isabel exclaimed.

"I know!" said Sparkle indignantly.

They laughed together until Isabel said curiously, "What were you doing at my school? Were you waiting for me?"

"Yes," said Sparkle. "I've found a

new home for the butterflies."

"Where? Will I still be able to visit them?" asked Isabel eagerly.

"Oh yes," said Sparkle, her eyes twinkling mischievously. "It's your garden."

"My garden?" Isabel was astounded. "But it's so small and there nothing in it."

"Butterflies don't need that much room," said Sparkle. "They need flowers. We can move the flowers growing here to your garden. They're going to be bulldozed when the builders start work. We'll move the plants whole, roots and all. So what do you think? Can the butterflies come and live with you?"

"It's a brilliant idea!" Isabel's face shone with excitement. "When can we start?"

"Now," said Sparkle.

She fluttered off Isabel's hand and flew to a clump of purple knapweed surrounded by butterflies. A pearly-white butterfly flew closer and tapped Sparkle on the wing. Sparkle shook her head.

"Sorry, but I can't play today. I've got a job to do."

Puzzled, the butterfly tapped Sparkle again then flew in the air, hovering above her.

Sparkle shook her head, hoping that when the butterfly saw her working she would understand. She was about to start her spell to dig up the knapweed when Isabel stopped her.

"How are you going to get the plants to my house?"

Sparkle wiggled her wings with embarrassment. She'd forgotten to ask Isabel if she'd carry them.

"We've got a wheelbarrow somewhere," said Isabel thoughtfully. "I think it's in the shed. I'll go home and look for it."

Isabel set off, her school bag bouncing on her back. Sparkle turned to the knapweed, clenching her wand while she worked out a spell to dig it up. Eventually she had one and, pointing the wand at the purple-headed plant, she chanted:

"Dig up this plant, its leaves and shoots,
Purple flowers and all its roots."

Immediately the wand grew warm and
the cluster of diamonds set in the gold star
sparkled and shone. The wand began to
hiss then a stream of red stars burst from it,
tumbling over the knapweed and making
it glitter. With a creaking noise the plant
started to move backwards and forwards.
The butterflies flew up in the air, their
colourful wings fluttering wildly. The plant
rocked faster and faster until, with a loud
ripping sound, its roots burst from the soil.

"Hooray," cheered Sparkle.

Next she pointed her wand at a
sprawling plant with large yellow daisy-
like flowers. It was hard work using magic
to dig up the flowers. Sparkle stopped for a
rest as Isabel returned, triumphantly pushing

a wheelbarrow with
a spade in it. The
butterflies that
had been hovering
overhead fluttered
away.

"Don't worry,"
said Sparkle
reassuringly. "They're
quite shy but they'll
come back when they
realize we're only *moving*
the plants."

"I hope you're right," said Isabel. "I
thought I'd help," she added, pointing at
the spade.

It took a long time to fill up the
wheelbarrow with plants, but at last Isabel
and Sparkle set off for Isabel's home.

"Luckily it's not too far," panted Isabel

as she pushed the wheelbarrow across the bumpy paving slabs.

Sparkle flew alongside her, calling out words of encouragement.

"I used to help Mum and Dad in the garden all the time at our old house," said Isabel, skilfully steering the barrow through

the side gate of her new home. She set it
down on the small patio. The flowerbed
was overgrown with weeds so Sparkle
used a little magic to help Isabel clear it.
Isabel squeaked with delight as the weeds
disappeared in a shower of red stars.

"Don't forget the stinging nettles," she
said, pointing to an untidy patch of green
plants.

Sparkle shook her head.

"Butterflies like to lay their eggs on
stinging nettles," she said.

Isabel looked at the plants with new
interest.

"I never knew stinging nettles were good
for butterflies. I've always hated them for
being ugly and because they sting. Mum's
right, then. She's always saying not to judge
things by the way they look."

Sparkle stared at Isabel, remembering

that Miss Alaska had said something similar to her last night.

Isabel set to work digging holes, filling them with water from the garden tap, placing the wild flowers in them and refilling the holes with soil. When Isabel had finished, the garden looked lovely but there was something missing. Butterflies! Hovering above the plants, Sparkle waved her wand:

"Butterflies please come and settle
In your new home of flowers and nettles."

Sparkle's wand hissed loudly and a flurry of red flower-scented stars cascaded over the plants. The stars sparkled and slowly dissolved in the afternoon sunshine. Then, as if holding its breath, the garden fell silent.

"What's that?" whispered Isabel, pointing

at a huge multicoloured cloud that seemed to be moving closer. The cloud hung over Isabel's garden for a moment and then dramatically split apart.

"Hooray!" shouted Isabel, realizing the cloud had been hundreds of brightly coloured butterflies.

Sparkle somersaulted with delight.

"We did it!" she cried. "We gave the butterflies a new home."

Chapter Seven

More butterflies kept arriving until there wasn't a petal's space left to spare. Most of the newcomers hovered in the air, waiting for a turn on the flowers but a few pushy ones chased the smaller butterflies away.

"It's just like school," said Isabel crossly. "There's always at least one bully. We'll have to go back to the wasteland and dig up more flowers so there's room for everyone."

Sadly Sparkle shook her head.

"There aren't any flowers left to move

– only a flowering bush that was too big for your garden. I don't recognize all these butterflies. Maybe they've come from somewhere else."

Isabel fell silent, her hair flopping over her face and her eyes screwing up with concentration.

"I've got an idea," she said at last. "There's a big DIY store near here. I went there last weekend with Mum and Dad to get some stuff for the house. It sells garden plants too. I could use my pocket money to buy more plants. I've been saving for ages so I've got quite a bit. We could fill up the empty spaces in the flower bed, and the pots and window boxes at the front of the house."

Sparkle was amazed at Isabel's generosity. "Are you sure you don't mind spending your money on plants?" she asked.

"I'd love to," said Isabel excitedly. "It'll be much nicer living here with a butterfly garden. And the flowers might attract other wildlife as well."

Isabel ran inside to collect her purse then Sparkle rode on her shoulder to the DIY store. Isabel kept giggling.

"Your wings are tickling my neck," she complained.

"I can fly if it's annoying you," said Sparkle.

"No," said Isabel. "I like it."

Isabel was very different from the day Sparkle had seen her in the magic mirror. Her eyes danced with happiness, especially when she was choosing flowers for her new garden. Sparkle helped, pointing out the types she knew butterflies were particularly fond of. As Isabel pushed her trolley full of plants to the check out, she had a thought.

"How will I get this lot home?" she whispered to Sparkle, who was hiding in a plant.

"Are you all right? Did you lose your mum and dad?" asked the lady at the check out, hearing her whispering.

76

"Mum and Dad aren't here," said Isabel. "I'm doing up the garden as a surprise for them."

"What a lovely thing to do." The lady beamed at Isabel. "If you promise to bring the trolley back, then you can borrow it to take your plants home."

"I promise," said Isabel solemnly.

It was getting late by the time Isabel and Sparkle had planted the new flowers. The garden was transformed. It was bright, colourful and alive with butterflies.

"It reminds me of living in the country," sighed Isabel happily.

Sparkle was excited too. Not only had she completed her first task but she'd helped Isabel. She turned three somersaults, making her new friend laugh. The back door opened and Isabel's parents appeared, side by side with enormous grins on their faces.

"Isabel," said her mum, coming outside. "What a lovely surprise! You've planted flowers in the pots at the front of the house and just look at the back garden too. And you did it all on your own!"

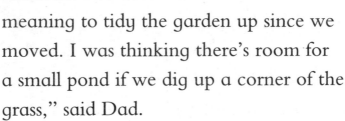

"Well, sort of," said Isabel, hiding a grin as Sparkle dived behind a flower.

"Isabel, this is fantastic. I've been meaning to tidy the garden up since we moved. I was thinking there's room for a small pond if we dig up a corner of the grass," said Dad.

"A pond!" exclaimed Isabel. "Then we might get frogs."

"And dragonflies," said Dad. "Tell

you what. I'll just change out of my work clothes and we'll nip down to the DIY shop and see if they've got any pond stuff."

"Can we?" said Isabel. "Thanks, Dad. I'll return the trolley I borrowed at the same time."

"I'll come too," said Mum, enthusiastically. "I'll just go put some jeans on."

As the back door closed, Sparkle flew out of hiding.

"Are you coming with us?" asked Isabel. "Please say yes."

"I've got to go home," said Sparkle sadly. It would have been fun to watch Isabel and her parents choose the things they needed for a pond.

Isabel pulled a sad face.

"Will I see you again?"

"Yes," said Sparkle. She definitely

wanted to come back to visit Isabel and to check up on her wildlife garden. "It might not be for ages, but I will come back."

Isabel grinned. "I'm looking forward to it already! Thanks for everything, Sparkle. If it hadn't been for you, none of this would have happened."

Blushing, Sparkle fluttered her wings.

"We did it together," she said.

"Friends forever?" asked Isabel.

"Definitely," Sparkle replied. She swept her wand in the air and, closing her eyes, murmured the friendship spell she'd learned in Cub Class.

> *"From me to you,*
> *A star that's true."*

The wand almost jerked out of her paw as an enormous red star burst from it. Sparkle

caught the star between her
paws and handed it to
Isabel.

"A friendship star
to remember me
by," she said.

"Thank you!
It's beautiful,"
Isabel thanked
her.

Dad appeared at
the back door. "Isabel, are you ready?"

Isabel hid the star in her pocket.

"Bye, Sparkle. See you again one day."

"Bye, Isabel."

Sparkle flew in the air and was about to
fly home when an enormous butterfly with
orange-and-black wings flitted past. Sparkle
couldn't help but stare. That was the most
beautiful butterfly she'd ever seen. A smaller

butterfly thought so too and shyly squeaked a greeting. The large butterfly ignored the smaller one and, landing on a petal, vainly spread out her wings.

"Looks aren't everything," remembered Sparkle, dipping her wings at the smaller butterfly.

The little butterfly dipped his wings in a friendly salute back.

"It's what's on the inside that counts," finished Sparkle, smiling to herself as she headed home.

Sparkle

1. Favourite colour – *red*

    2. Favourite gemstone – *ruby*

3. Best flower – *rose*

    4. Cutest animal – *foal*

5. Birthday month – *June*

    6. Yummiest food – *nectar*

7. Favourite place – *the Butterfly Bridge*

    8. Hobbies – *dancing*

9. Best ever season – *summer*

    10. Worst thing – *bedtime*

Sparkle's Wordsnake

Helping the butterflies was hard work but it felt so great to find them a new home and pass my task! See if you can find all the words below hidden in my winding wordsnake. The words go in one continuous line, up and down, backwards and forwards, but never diagonally.

```
S  P  A  S  E
L  K  R  I  M
E  D  I  R  O
O  M  A  P  S
N  S  T  A  R
D  N  E  D  R
B  U  T  G  A
R  E  T  K  S
F  L  Y  T  A
```

SPARKLE   DIAMOND   BUTTERFLY
TASK   GARDEN   STARS   PROMISE

A Puzzle for Primrose

Brainy Primrose is stuck! Her task is to help a sad little dog, but she keeps seeing Lucy in the magic mirror. Will she solve the puzzle in time?

Misty Makes Friends

Caring Misty must help Jessica and her stepsister Becky to become friends. But first Misty must realize that being confident isn't easy for everyone . . .

Collect tokens from each Fairy Bears book to WIN!

What prizes can you get?

3 tokens get a Fairy Bears colour poster for your wall!

5 tokens get a sheet of super-cute Fairy Bears stickers!

8 tokens get a set of postcards to send to your friends, plus a certificate signed by the Fairy Bears creator, Julie Sykes!

Send them in as soon as you get them or wait and collect more for a bigger and better prize!

Send in the correct number of tokens, along with your name, address and parent's/guardian's signature (you must get your parent's/guardian's signature to take part in this offer) to: Fairy Bears Collection, Marketing Dept, Macmillan Children's Books, 20 New Wharf Road, London N1 9RR.

Terms and conditions: Open to UK and Eire residents only. Purchase of the Fairy Bears books is necessary. Please ask permission of your parent/guardian to enter this offer. The correct number of tokens must be included for the offer to be redeemed. No group entries allowed. Photocopied tokens will not be accepted. Prizes are distributed on a first come, first served basis, while stocks last. No part of the offer is exchangeable for cash or any other offer. Please allow 28 days for delivery. We will use your data only for the purpose of fulfilling this offer. We will not pass information on to any third parties. All data will be destroyed after the promotion. For full terms and conditions, write to: Fairy Bears Collection, Marketing Dept, Macmillan Children's Books, 20 New Wharf Road, London N1 9RR or visit www.fairybearsworld.com

Fairy Bears Token Offer

1 Token

Prizes available while stocks last. See www.fairybearsworld.com for more details

Fairy Bears Token Offer

1 Token

Prizes available while stocks last. See www.fairybearsworld.com for more details

Fairy Bears

By Julie Sykes

Discover more friendly Fairy Bears!

Dizzy	978-0-330-51201-5	£3.99
Sunny	978-0-330-51202-2	£3.99
Blossom	978-0-330-51203-9	£3.99
Sparkle	978-0-330-51204-6	£3.99
Primrose	978-0-330-51205-3	£3.99
Misty	978-0-330-51206-0	£3.99
Lulu	978-0-330-51207-7	£3.99
Poppy	978-0-330-51208-4	£3.99

The prices shown above are correct at the time of going to press. However, Macmillan Publishers reserves the right to show new retail prices on covers, which may differ from those previously advertised.

All Pan Macmillan titles can be ordered from our website, www.panmacmillan.com, or from your local bookshop and are also available by post from:

Bookpost, PO Box 29, Douglas, Isle of Man IM99 1BQ

Credit cards accepted. For details:
Telephone: 01624 677237
Fax: 01624 670923
Email: bookshop@enterprise.net
www.bookpost.co.uk

Free postage and packing in the United Kingdom